Caring for Outdoor Places

Heather Hammonds

Contents

Chapter 1	**Outdoor Fun**	2
Chapter 2	**Sharing the Environment**	4
Chapter 3	**In the Forest**	6
Chapter 4	**On the Beach**	12
Chapter 5	**At the Park**	18
Chapter 6	**A Helping Hand**	22
Glossary and Index		24

Chapter 1

Outdoor Fun

Do you enjoy visiting outdoor places? You can have a picnic or barbecue in the outdoors.

You can also get lots of exercise and fresh air as you explore your surroundings.

Many interesting facts can also be learned about the plants and animals that live in the places you visit.

Outdoor places are very beautiful.

You can hike among tall trees and see lots of **wildlife** when you visit a forest.

When you visit a beach you can explore rock pools, walk along the sandy shore and watch the waves.

You can sit by a lake or admire the flowers in a park.

Central Park, New York, U.S.A.

This beautiful park is in the middle of a big city.

Chapter 2

Sharing the Environment

Forests, beaches and parks are home to lots of animals. Some animals you may see or hear. Other animals may be very shy.

It is exciting to learn about the animals that live in these places. They are usually different from the animals that live near your home.

gulls

kangaroos

When you visit forests, beaches and parks, you share them with the animals that live there.

It is important to look after these special places, so that they are not damaged by people visiting them. Then the animals will continue to live in them.

Signs at forests, beaches and parks remind you to take care of them.

Chapter 3
In the Forest

Tom and Matt like to visit the forest. While they hike along the forest paths, birds sing from the treetops. They see forest animals running through the trees.

Sometimes, Tom and Matt have a picnic or barbecue in the forest too.

When Tom and Matt go hiking in the forest, they always keep to the paths. This helps protect the small plants growing under the trees.

Tom and Matt do not make loud noises when they hike through the forest. Then the animals that live in the forest are not **disturbed**.

Never pick plants or their flowers when you visit a forest. Flowers often turn into seeds, which grow into new plants. Many plants are food for forest animals.

When Tom and Matt have a picnic in the forest, they take home all their rubbish and food scraps.

Leaving rubbish behind litters the forest. Forest animals sometimes eat food scraps. The food scraps can be bad for the forest animals.

Some picnic sites have bins.

When Tom and Matt's family and friends have a barbecue in the forest, they use the barbecues at picnic sites. They never take wood from the forest to make a fire.

Some animals make their homes in old, dead trees. Insects live in fallen tree branches.

Lighting camp fires in a forest can be very dangerous!

Focus on Rivers and Streams

Rivers and streams flow through most forests. Forest animals get drinking water from them.

Water birds and other animals live beside the rivers and streams. They hunt for food in the water.

Many kinds of fish live in rivers and streams too.

Platypus live beside rivers and streams in eastern Australia. They dig long burrows beside the rivers and streams, and hunt for food in the water.

Beavers live in rivers, streams, lakes and ponds in North America. Beavers make dams in the water and live in **lodges** behind the dams.

Platypus and beavers often live beside rivers and streams in forests, where it is quiet and they are not disturbed by people.

Chapter 4

On the Beach

Maria and Nina like to visit the beach with their parents.

At **low tide**, they walk on the rocks and explore rock pools. When the weather is warm, they swim in the sea.

They use their mum's **binoculars** to watch sea birds hunting for food.

Maria and Nina walk across sand dunes to get to their favourite beach. They always keep to the path and stay inside the fences on the sand dunes. They never play on the sand dunes. Sand dunes are easily **eroded** by people walking or playing on them.

magellanic penguins

Lots of small plants grow on sand dunes and help hold them together. Animals make their homes in sand dunes too.

When Maria and Nina explore rock pools, they do not take shells, rocks or seaweed from them.

Water creatures live in shells, under rocks and among the seaweed.

Maria and Nina also find beautiful shells on the beach. They leave them where they find them, so others can enjoy them too.

Sometimes Maria's and Nina's dad goes fishing. He keeps his fishing line and fish hooks safely in a box. He never leaves old fishing line or fish hooks behind. Old fishing line and fish hooks can harm sea birds and other animals.

Plastic bags and other rubbish can also be very harmful to sea birds and other animals.

Focus on Shorebirds

Shorebirds build nests close to water places, such as the sea or **wetlands.**

Some shorebirds live in one area all year round. They do not travel far from the places where they nest.

Other shorebirds fly thousands of kilometres from country to country at different times of the year.

pied oystercatchers

Hooded plovers nest on beaches in south-eastern Australia. They lay their eggs in shallow nests, called **scrapes**.

Western snowy plovers nest on beaches in the western United States. They also lay their eggs in scrapes.

Hooded plovers and western snowy plovers are **endangered** shorebirds.

a hooded plover

a western snowy plover

The nests of endangered shorebirds are hard to see. They are often accidentally damaged by people or dogs.

Chapter 5

At the Park

Tamara and Helen live in a big city. Every weekend they visit their **local** park.

Water birds make their homes on and around the park lake. Butterflies and bees fly around the flowers in the park. Blackbirds build their nests in the trees.

Tamara and Helen enjoy watching the wildlife in the park.

Sometimes Tamara and Helen take their dog to the park. They read the park signs to see where she must be kept on her lead, and only take her to areas where dogs are allowed.

Then she won't disturb the birds and other animals that live in the park.

City parks provide places for birds to live and breed. Without the parks, many of the birds could not live in the city.

Focus on Park Lakes and Ponds

Many city parks have beautiful lakes and ponds.

Ducks, swans and other water birds can be seen on them. Tadpoles sometimes swim in the water and frogs croak from their hiding places among the water plants.

Thousands of insects fly above the lakes and ponds too.

Eels live in some park lakes and ponds. Eels are long, thin fish with short fins. Some eels grow more than a metre long!

Turtles live in and around some park lakes and ponds too. They eat water plants and other small water creatures.

It is important to keep litter out of park lakes and ponds. Fish, such as eels, and other water animals need clean water to survive.

Chapter 6
A Helping Hand

You can help look after your favourite outdoor place by joining an **environmental group**.

Environmental groups hold clean-up days. They collect litter left by careless visitors.

Environmental groups also hold tree-planting days. They plant lots of trees and other plants.

Some environmental groups also help endangered animals. Group members watch over the animals. They teach others about them too.

Environmental groups work hard to protect the world's special outdoor places.

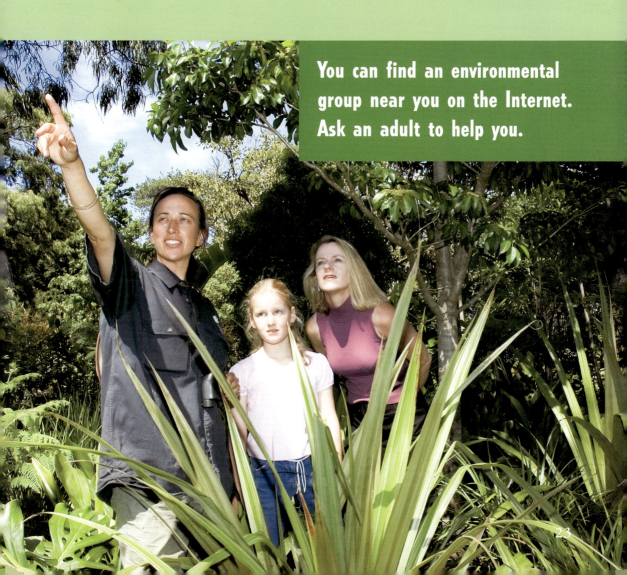

You can find an environmental group near you on the Internet. Ask an adult to help you.

Glossary

binoculars — two small telescopes joined together, which are used to make things that are far away look closer

disturbed — scared, bothered or interfered with

endangered — when something is in danger of being killed, or dying out

environmental group — a group of people who work to look after our environment, and the plants and animals in it

eroded — worn away

local — close to home

lodges — homes of sticks, mud and stones built by beavers

low tide — the time on the seashore when the sea has gone down, and more of the beach can be seen

scrapes — small hollows in the ground made by some birds and used as nests

wetlands — places where water meets the land, such as marshes, swamps and lakes

wildlife — animals that are not tame, and live in outdoor places

Index

beavers 11
dogs 19
eels 21
environmental groups 22, 23
hiking 3, 6, 7

hooded plovers 17
platypus 11
sand dunes 13
turtles 21
western snowy plovers 17